The Lion and

by Eriko Kishida
Illustrated by
Chiyoko Nakatani

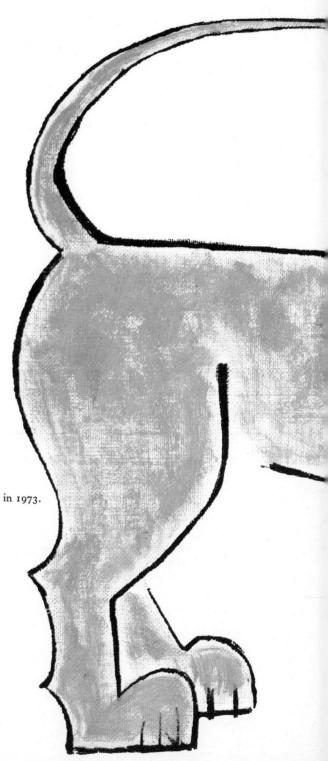

First published in the United States of America in 1973.
L.C. Card 72-76822
ISBN 0-690-49502-1
0-690-49503-X (LB)
Printed in Great Britain

Thomas Y. Crowell
Company

New York

Jojo was the strongest of all the
lions. He was King of the Jungle.
When he walked through the
forest, with the sun glinting on
his crown, all the other animals
were afraid. They ran and hid
from him. They did not know
that . . .

he was growing old. He was tired of
chasing zebras. He was tired of
everything. He went to the river to
have a drink of water and a little rest.

As he looked at himself in the water
Jojo realized that he could no longer see
himself clearly.

"Oh, dear," he said sadly, "my eyes are growing dim with age. I'm not much of a King anymore."

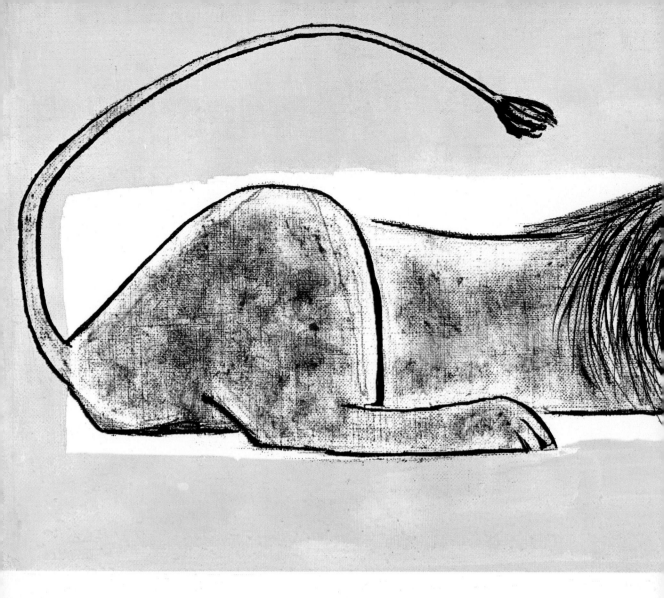

Just then a small bird landed on
the ground beside him.

"King Jojo, you look as sad as
I am," said the bird.

"Why are you sad?" asked Jojo.

"Because I have lost my six
lovely eggs. A leopard stole three

of them, two were swallowed by
a snake, and the last one fell
into the river."

"You poor bird," said Jojo.

"What you need is a safe place
to lay your eggs. Perhaps I can
help you. Would you like to use
my crown?"

"What a wonderful idea!" The little bird hopped up and down with excitement. "My eggs would be quite safe in your crown."

So the little bird built a new nest in Jojo's crown and laid seven new eggs in it. Now when Jojo walked through the forest, he stepped very carefully. He carried a precious burden on his head.

When it rained Jojo sat
quietly under a big tree
so that the bird and her
eggs would not get wet,
and she stayed there
until the storm was over.

At night the bird and
the lion slept very well.
They were not afraid of
anything. Neither the
leopard nor the snake would
dare to steal eggs from
the King of the Jungle.

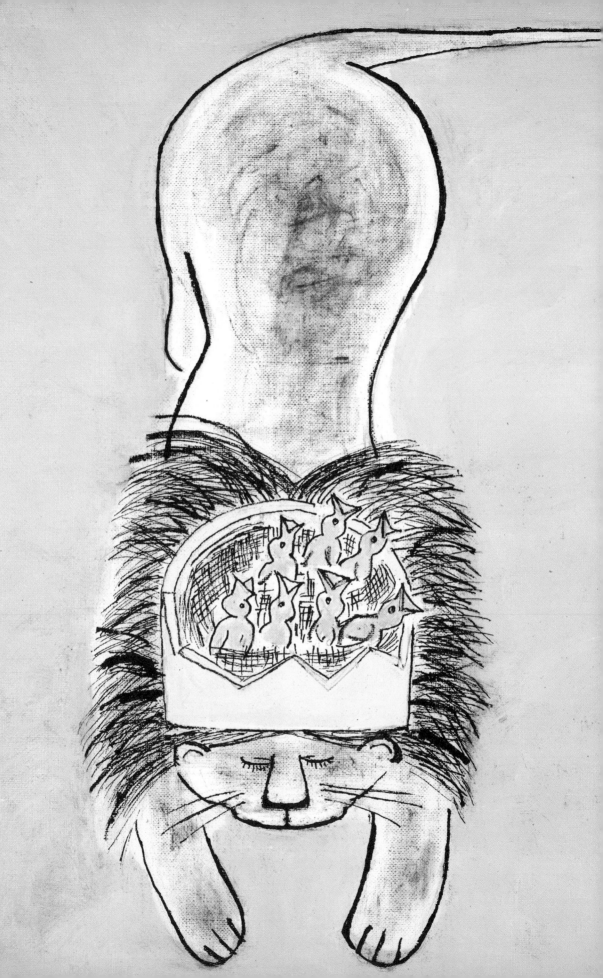

When spring came the eggs
hatched, one by one. Seven
baby birds chirped loudly in
their special nest. All day long
their mother was kept busy
feeding them.

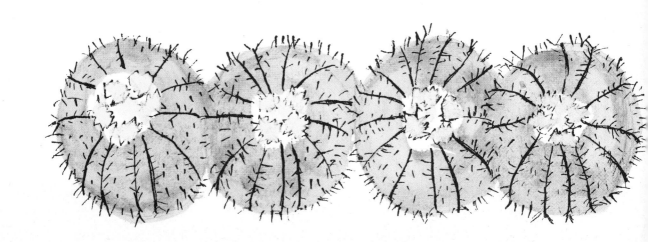

When they grew old enough to
fly, the little birds did not leave
Jojo. They stayed near him and
looked after him. And the great
lion was happy to sit in the sun
with his poor eyes closed and
listen to the birds singing.

Soon the other animals of the
forest saw how gentle their King
Jojo had become. They never ran
away from him again.